ESCAPADE JOHNSON
and
THE COFFEE SHOP
OF THE
LIVING DEAD

written by
Michael Sullivan

illustrated by
Joy Kolitsky

W9-CMM-915

PUBLISHINGWORKS, INC.
EXETER, NH
2008

INTRODUCTION

As a rule, I don't get into a whole lot of trouble. It's not that I'm a real goodie-goodie, I just don't always jump at the chance when it comes along. I'll see an opportunity to do something really cool, and while I'm thinking about doing it, the chance just sort of goes away. Now Davy Gilman, he never misses a chance to get into trouble. He's never stopped to think about anything in his life.

That's how it all started, the trouble with the Coffee Shop of the Living Dead. It was Davy who stumbled into the mess, and I just fell in with him. And then, of course, there was Jimmy Whitehorse, just itching to dive on in too. I suppose I shouldn't be surprised that any story that starts out with me, Davy, and Jimmy walking down the street together is going to end up with me grounded, in deadly danger, or running from the cops. I haven't been in that much trouble since I rewired my family's satellite dish and started picking up my principal's cell phone calls to her psychiatrist. But that's another story.

This one is about a homework strike, three generations of bulldogs, a dancing espresso machine, and the Coffee Shop of the Living Dead.

Enjoy.

CHAPTER 1

Davy and I were walking home from school together, which should tell you what kind of day I was having. Davy and I have never gotten along, not since we met in kindergarten when Davy proved Legos are not indestructible by using my newly built Lego castle as an example.

Davy is a big guy, or a small rhinoceros, take your pick. When he stomps on things, they stay stomped. Legos, toes, bugs, lunchboxes. He once got mad at Jimmy Whitehorse's doghouse for not getting out of the way of his speeding bicycle and then stomped that doghouse into wood pulp. Jimmy was just glad he got his dog out before the roof caved in.

Davy and I were walking home together because we had a history project to do. We had to do it together because we were the only two fifth-graders at Sanbornton Elementary School who didn't do it when it was assigned. Benny Black may not have done a very good job of it, but even he turned in something and passed.

"Living history?" Davy was saying. "That's the dumbest thing I ever heard."

"What do you mean? You've said three things today that were dumber than that," declared Jimmy Whitehorse as he dropped out of a tree limb onto Davy's shoulders and then bounced off onto the ground. Davy didn't flinch. Jimmy ended up with his head stuck in a bush.

"Traitor!" Davy snarled at Jimmy's butt. "What happened to, 'Mrs. Bartgauer can't punish us all if nobody does the homework,' huh?"

"Aw, you knew Cherilyn and Katrina at least were gonna bail. It was a dumb idea to begin with."

It was October, and Davy had been doing homework for two months, since the beginning of school. All right, to be honest, he had been avoiding homework for two months. He had run out of excuses in a week. Our teacher, Mrs. Bartgauer, figured out he was forging notes from his parents a week later. Since then, he had been taking an F on every homework assignment. He had to do something. Of course, I suggested he do his homework, but it turns out that was a stupid suggestion. Instead, he organized the Great Fifth Grade Homework Strike. He told everyone in our class to skip doing our social studies homework on the same day. If none of us handed anything in, he argued, what could Mrs. Bartgauer do? If she graded on a curve, then we would all get C's, right? He either convinced, or threatened, everyone into doing it…at least he thought he did.

As a matter of fact, the Great Fifth Grade Homework Strike actually resulted in more homework being done than ever. On any given day, ten or more fifth-graders were handing in lame excuses instead of homework. But Mrs. Bartgauer had gotten wind of what was up. The day before the strike, she stood at the blackboard, a tall, wide, powerful looking woman in her trademark flowered cotton dress. She wrote threats on the blackboard, terrible, gruesome, and surprisingly specific threats. In the end, only Davy and I had shown up without the latest assignment.

"And what's up with you?" Jimmy asked, laughing. He got his feet back on the ground and his head back up in the air, then punched me in the arm. "Escapade the rebel, I wouldn't have believed it if I hadn't seen it with my own two ears."

I shrugged and tried to look cool. These guys didn't need to know that I didn't have the heart to ask my parents about the last three generations of their families. My parents hated to talk about their own families, although they had no problem talking about each other's. What they said, I couldn't hand in to Mrs. Bartgauer. I had joined the boycott on pure wishful thinking that I would get out of the assignment.

"What's up with me?" I yelled at Jimmy. "What's up with you? You haven't done homework in a month, why now?"

"Finally got an assignment I was interested in."

"Three generations of family members?"

"Yeah, Brutus, son of Mauler, son of Fiend."

There was a moment of disbelief. I couldn't decide if Jimmy was a genius or a bigger idiot than I had ever thought possible. What imagination, what inventiveness, what daring, what absolute insanity!

"Your dogs?" cried Davy. "You did your living history project on a bunch of stupid bulldogs?"

"Sure, they are part of the family. Brutus was a little hard to interview, but he had great stories of his old grandpa."

"And Mrs. Bartgauer bought that?" I asked, amazed.

"Hey, she was just happy to get anything

with the strike on. Easiest D I ever got," he said proudly.

"And now we have to not only do our relatives, but we have to compare and contrast them," moaned Davy. "Hey, Escapade, do you think I can compare your uncles to the family of skunks that lives under my porch?"

CHAPTER 2

The funny thing is I was actually starting to enjoy joking around with Davy and Jimmy. Maybe there was something to juvenile delinquency after all. It was certainly more fun complaining about Mrs. Bartgauer now that I was on her bad side.

It's not that Mrs. Bartgauer is hard to annoy, it's just that the line to get on her bad side was pretty long now that she was teaching my class.

It was only a month into school and already Marjorie Jackson had managed to get the cord to the classroom computer stuck in the electric pencil sharpener, someone had filled the legs of Benny Black's jeans with toothpaste during gym class, and someone had dropped a fake snake on Mrs. Bartgauer's head halfway up a mountain. And that's saying nothing compared to what Jimmy Whitehorse's parents had done to her. They were famous for their pranks during parent-teacher conferences, but they still managed to convince Mrs. Bartgauer that their son was a carrier of a rare tropical disease that causes limbs to turn black and fall off. I don't think she would have bought it if Jimmy's feet didn't smell like they were rotting already.

Now, though, I had made it in to the crowded realm of Mrs. Bartgauer's bad side. Who would have guessed that a little thing like a homework strike would be such a big deal to a teacher? I was just pointing out to Jimmy and Davy that adults were supposed to have more patience than that when we came to where School Street met Main Street. We had just cut through the parking lot of Joe's Cup of Joe, the only coffee shop in all of Sanbornton, when we stopped dead in our tracks. It wasn't because we wanted a cup of coffee. Kids didn't go into that coffee shop, ever. No, what made us freeze was the sight of Cherilyn Travis and Katrina Finink just reaching the intersection from Main Street.

Jimmy's eyes locked on Katrina, tall and raven-haired, and always looking even taller in her long, straight skirts. She towered a full foot over Jimmy, and his neck was likely permanently damaged from staring up at her. Davy and I seldom noticed Katrina, because she was always standing beside Cherilyn. Cherilyn was every fifth-grade boy's dream, in her pink bows, pink sneakers, pink skirts, and streamlined silver braces. She was the first girl in my class to get contact lenses, and they were a bright purple! Moisture seemed to pour out of me, from pores, armpits, and saliva glands, anytime I got within five feet of her. Jimmy and I were speechless; Davy could only manage a ground-shaking belch.

"Aren't you supposed to be wearing your orange prison overalls?" called out Cherilyn, stopping to look at the three of us standing bug-eyed. "Really, I don't know how they expect us responsible members of society to feel safe with the likes of you running around free."

"Me neither," said Katrina, stopping to add her agreement to whatever Cherilyn said as she always did.

That may not have snapped Davy out of his stupor, but the sudden shower from the coffee shop's sprinkler system coming on did. Me? It would have taken a tidal wave to move me right then. Davy dove for the nearest sprinkler head and pressed his thumb down on it, sending a geyser of water that hit his target with amazing accuracy.

Katrina and Cherilyn screamed and took off down the sidewalk, but they didn't get far.

Jimmy found his own sprinkler head and cut them off. They were trapped, with waterfalls on either side, the road behind them, and us in front. Katrina turned bright red then raised her hands, fingers extended into claws. Cherilyn clenched her hands into fists and took a step forward.

I don't know what it was that made me do it. Maybe it was the warm, chummy feeling from hanging out with the guys, maybe it was some warped need to be noticed brought on by Cherilyn's sea green sweater, or maybe I just felt like stopping Katrina's fingernails from reaching me while I still had two good eyeballs. For whatever reason, I dove onto a sprinkler head, bent it forward, and pressed my thumb over the top three-quarters of the opening. The water shot forward like a fire hose. Davy's targets had been moving away from him. My targets were moving right at me. An easy shot!

"Escapade, I'm going to –" Katrina yelled, sputtering through the shower of water that had caught her head-on. But she never got to finish her sentence because too many things happened at once. The built-up water pressure suddenly burst out, sending spouts of water straight up in the air from half a dozen other sprinkler heads. Jimmy leapt for the spigot to turn off the water, but, in his excitement, pulled the handle clean off. Cherilyn and Katrina reversed direction and ran out into the street. A car swerved. (Can you imagine? Not one car an hour came down that street and it had to be right then.) It jumped the curve, cut across the sidewalk, skidded up the wet grass, and flattened the coffee shop's wooden sign. Mr. Patchani, the owner of the coffee shop, leapt out of the car, his mouth moving, but nothing coming out. I think he was so mad he was having trouble breathing.

The crashing, the screeching, and the splintering of wood all died down, and there was a momentary silence as everyone involved reassessed the situation. Jimmy found himself standing in the middle of a disaster and holding an incriminating metal spigot handle. He quickly tossed it over his shoulder without paying any attention to where he threw it. The silence was broken by a loud crash and the gentle tinkling of glass as the coffee shop's picture window disintegrated into a thousand shards.

CHAPTER 3

"Five hundred and sixty-eight dollars! That's what it would cost to make this right." My dad was pacing back and forth in the kitchen, his clenched fists pounding against his thighs. I had never seen him so mad. For eleven years I stayed out of trouble, well, except when I accidentally fed the police chief's coat into the pasta machine at the school's international dinner, but that wasn't really my fault.

Come to think of it, this wasn't my fault either! I was just following Davy's lead, and it was Jimmy who broke the window.

"Dad, I…"

"Don't even think about claiming this wasn't your fault!" Dad warned. This guy really knew his stuff.

Mom was sitting at the table across from me. She kept reaching out to touch my hands or my shoulder, but pulled back before she made contact. My little sister Revelation (yes, real name, no weirder than mine) was peeking around the doorframe from the living room, giggling at how much trouble I was in.

"Well," I mumbled hopefully, "at least my third of that won't be too bad."

"That IS your third of it!" my dad roared.

"Oh." I decided I was unlikely to help matters by saying anything more.

"What were you thinking? Someone could have been killed."

"You could have been killed," my mom added, sounding more thoughtful than worried.

"That was probably the least of his worries," my dad said, facing the kitchen window. My mom seemed to think about that for a second, and then, to my horror, nodded in agreement. Even she wasn't going to soften this for me. I decided maybe I did have to talk my way out of this one.

"I'll pay it off. I swear. I'll get a job and pay back every penny."

Dad spun around. The muscles on his face twitching. I thought something on his forehead might burst. I hadn't seen him this mad since I brought home a skunk and gave it to Revelation as a pet. His words came out through clenched teeth.

"You'll get a job, huh? How? You're eleven. Are you going to pick up a few extra shifts driving a Greyhound bus?"

"First your history homework, now this...." My mom was almost crying, clearly not keeping up with the conversation.

"I don't know," I babbled, desperately trying to think. "I'll collect newspapers, I'll mow lawns —" I knew it was the wrong thing to say before it even came out of my mouth.

"Oh yeah," my dad scoffed. "Gardening, that's what we want you doing. That's how you got into this mess in the first place."

I don't know why I thought my dad was somehow above sarcasm. Clearly, I hadn't been paying attention.

"No," he said, his voice suddenly dropping to something just above a whisper. "I already know how you are going to work this off." Which was worse, I had to wonder, the steam-coming-out-of-his-ears-charging-bull dad, or this scary-calm-you've-already-sat-in-the-electric-chair-and-all-I-have-to-do-is-throw-the-switch dad? I didn't like either of them.

"At your work?" I interrupted, hopefully. My dad manages a video store in the next town over, and he always has movies showing on the television screens hanging from the ceiling and video games out for people to try.

"No, your punishment is not going to be free video games every afternoon."

I was a little amazed at how well he knew me. All those news reports we have to watch in current events say parents are supposed to be detached these days. Why did I have to get Super Dad?

"Your mother and I sat down with Mr. Patchani and the parents of those other…boys," he growled. "Mr. Patchani agreed not to call the police in on this." He glanced at my mom, who dispatches for the county sheriff's department. She looked pale at just the mention of the cops, HER guys, getting their hands on her son. "He wants you to be responsible, but he knows you boys are too young to get regular jobs, so he's agreed to let you work your debts off at the coffee shop."

It was my turn to look ill, or at least I guess I must have looked ill because I felt like I was about to throw up.

"Not there, Dad. Please! Do you know what they call that place?"

Dad looked blank. He looked at Mom, who shook her head, then back at me. How could they be so out of it? How could they not know about the great evil in their midst? I swallowed hard, afraid even to say the words.

"They call it the Coffee Shop of the Living Dead!"

CHAPTER 4

The next day I had to get straight home after school to go to Concord with my parents. There was this special form that my parents had to sign at some state office before I could work, even for nothing. Anyone under sixteen needed the form, and had to listen to this speech by a guy in a short-sleeved shirt and a tie. The speech was all about how this was great training for when I would become a productive member of the work force, and how earning a good day's pay for a good day's work was the greatest thing I could ever do. He went on and on and on and on. I swear, half the eleven-year-olds who went in to get the form wouldn't need it by the time the speech was over.

My parents didn't say a word to me the whole car ride to Concord and back. They acted like I wasn't there. Like I could be that lucky. I'd rather have been out on the basketball courts behind the school for my last day of freedom. Two hours per day, five days a week, at the rate

Mr. Patchani was paying, or not paying, me, it would take ten weeks to work off my share of the damage! It wasn't fair, I kept telling myself. It wasn't my idea; I would never have gotten into trouble like this on my own.

It would have made me feel better knowing that those guys would be working it off, too, except that meant I'd be working with them. Every minute would be a reminder of how I got into this mess in the first place. I never hang out with these guys, and then one afternoon I do, and I'm stuck with them forever. Would I have to put up with their stupid horsing around every day? Worse, would I start acting like them?

We somehow lived through the silent ride home, a silent hour when mom and dad made dinner and I did homework at the kitchen table, and a dinner that would have been silent if it weren't for my sister, Revelation. She took advantage of having no one interrupt her to chatter away the whole time.

"At kindergarten today, Jeremy was picking his nose during snack time, and I think he accidentally ate some…And at kindergarten today, Mrs. Howitzer got sooooo mad at Missy that she broke her ruler in her bare hands!…And at recess today we had to all stay inside and wash the hamster cage because someone poured Kool-Aid all over Mr. Fibble…And at kindergarten today, we learned how to draw a flower…And at snack today we had Rice Krispy treats that Molly's nana brought in…And at kindergarten today we learned that New Hampshire is a whole state, all by itself…Molly's nana is her grandma, that's what Molly calls her, nana…Mr. Fibble is a hamster…"

I guess if you are as young as she is, today seems pretty important because you don't have many days to compare it to.

Finally, dinner was over and dad stared at me until I cleared the dishes. Revelation walked into the living room to watch TV, still talking away at a million miles a minute. I started to follow, but my dad coughed so loudly in that special way that means, "Don't you dare walk away before we have a little talk young man." At least I think that's what it meant, so I sat back down at the table.

"OK, Escapade," Dad said. "I'll bite. Why do they call it the Coffee Shop of the Living Dead?"

I knew I never should have said that. Parents should always be kept on a need-to-know basis.

"It's just a name the kids use, like calling the fire department the Sanbornton Cellar Savers, or calling the police the Blue Birds of…"

Mom was glaring at me. Need-to-know, right. I shut up quick.

"Well," said Dad, "you kids call it that for a reason. You might as well tell us now."

I sat there for a whole minute, trying to look so miserable they would let me go. They didn't look like they were buying it. So I fessed up.

"It's…it's the old folks that work there. They've got to be like 140 years old. You can smell the old people smell from outside the door."

Mom and Dad looked at each other. They

both shrugged. Dad's shrug looked like a, "Do you know anything about this?" kind of shrug. Mom's was a little more like, "Beats me. I go to the coffee shop in Laconia near the dispatch center; I don't remember why."

It was Mom who spoke, slowly, carefully, in that voice she uses when she tells me something I should remember for the rest of my life. "Escapade, older people have a right to work too. That shop has always had older people working there. Even when I was a teenager the couple behind the counter was easily in their nineties. That's no reason to make fun of them, and it's no excuse for trying to get out of working there."

"But old age is contagious, isn't it? I mean, if I hang out with old people long enough, I'll get old too, won't I?"

Dad started to answer, then closed his mouth and opened it a few times without anything coming out. Mom gave him her extra-special, "He's your son, I'm just a spectator here," shrug and left the room. Dad flapped his gums a few more times, coughed, and walked away without a word.

There I was, all alone. I wasn't the one who wanted this little chat, anyway. Still, I was left to contemplate my fate. Tomorrow I would be handed over to the undead, doomed to endless hours of back-breaking work for my inhuman masters, with only a couple of cavemen for allies. How could my parents allow this? How could they abandon me? How could they have not called me when True Tales of the Los Angeles Police Dog Corps started ten minutes ago?

I got up to head to my regular seat in front of the living room TV.

"Wash the dishes!" my mom called from the living room couch. Oh, she knows me too well.

CHAPTER 5

All the next day I dreaded what was coming.
I couldn't even get excited when Benny slipped
a live mouse into Mr. Hauteman's, the science
teacher's, coffee mug. All right, I laughed a little

when he pulled his lips away from the mug with the mouse hanging from his mustache, but my heart really wasn't in it.

Periods flew by. Music, English, science, recess, lunch. I was so distracted in French class that I forgot to roll my r's in that way that made Ms. Jensen so happy. The end of school bell never came so fast before. Suddenly, it was all over. I looked desperately at Mrs. Bartgauer, thinking too late of the one person who could save me.

"Mrs. Bartgauer, I have to stay after school, right? I mean, didn't I do something wrong today?"

"Mr. Johnson, if you had to stay after school today then I would have to stay with you, and that's just not going to happen. I don't even care if you burned down the cafeteria, GO HOME!"

If only that's where I was going. Mrs. Bartgauer threw a pile of papers in her bag and stomped out of the room in a cloud of vibrating, flowered cotton. The time had come.

I trudged down School Street, my feet never lifting off the ground. Pebbles were working their way through the soles of my sneakers. Suddenly, there were Jimmy and Davy, punching each other, yelling insults, generally being their happy and friendly selves. How could they be so calm at a time like this?

"What's the matter, Escapade?" Jimmy yelled as Davy threw him into the upper branches of a pine tree, which immediately sagged over and dropped him on the ground. "You look like you just had to kiss Mrs. Bartgauer's... yow!"

Davy tossed him back to the top of the tree.

"What's the matter with me? What's the matter with you guys? Don't you get it? We're going to have to spend the next ten weeks in the Coffee Shop of the Living Dead!"

Davy looked down at Jimmy, who had just landed once more in the same spot. "Three days," he said confidently.

"Two, max," said Jimmy, scrambling back to his feet.

"No, ten weeks, that's what my folks agreed to."

"They'll be dying to get rid of us in less than an hour," Davy stated, with all the confidence of someone who had almost single-handedly convinced a twenty-seven year old teacher to retire rather than face a year teaching him.

Of course, that was it. Why was I so afraid of a couple of walking corpses when I had the pre-teen terminator on my side? I suddenly felt like I might have a future after all.

So the three of us walked confidently into Joe's Cup of Joe. We came face to face with Mr. Patchani holding a mop at his side like a rifle in the hands of a royal guard.

"You're late," he said without even a hello. Behind him, two figures stood frozen. No, not frozen, one of them moved, at least I think he moved. His hand was on the counter one minute, and the next it was a quarter of an inch above it. Now it was half an inch above the counter. He was definitely moving. You couldn't actually see him move, but if you looked hard enough, you could see more and more daylight between him and the laminated slab. I guess it was also possible the counter was slowly sinking away. Mr. Patchani was halfway through his speech before I came back to the present.

"…every day, I don't care if there is a hurricane. If any of you, any ONE of you, mess up this chance, all your names go to the police. Do I make myself clear?" His voice rose to a near-hysterical squeak.

Had I heard right? One screw-up and we all went down. Suddenly the confidence I had felt in the presence of two master delinquents drained away. I still didn't doubt that these guys could make pests of themselves, I just wasn't sure I wanted them to.

"This is Mr. Peterson." Mr. Patchani pointed towards the man behind the counter whose hand was almost raised high enough to be a wave. It's a good thing he got a head start.

"Mr. OOMP," Davy whispered under his breath.

"And this is Mrs. Peterson," Mr. Patchani added, pointing to the lady, who hadn't moved at all.

"Mrs. LUMP," Jimmy added, a bit louder than Davy. Mr. Patchani seemed to almost hear and almost snap back, but shook his head and went on.

Mr. Patchani continued, "They are the afternoon shift. You are their assistants. You do everything they tell you to do, and maybe I won't have the police send you to jail." With that threat hanging in the air, he stalked into his office and slammed the door.

I leaned over and whispered, "Mr. OOMP?"

Davy snickered. "Mr. OOMP: Old, Old Man Peterson."

"And Mrs. LUMP?"

It was Jimmy's turn. "Mrs. LUMP: Lady Undead Mrs. Peterson."

The two gave each other a high five and started to laugh, but went silent as a strange crackling noise seemed to materialize in the air. We all looked around thinking that wires were frying somewhere or the vinyl upholstery of the booths was being shredded by tiny claws. Finally, we realized the noise was coming from behind the counter. It was Mr. OOMP, and he was starting to speak.

CHAPTER 6

"**Y**ou...............b-b-boys.................

grab...........a......bbb..b..b...b......"

Mr. OOMP's arms moved up in front of him

and he started to sway back and forth.

"Broom?" I offered.

"M-m-m-op," he finally spat out and began panting slightly. "Mop................the...... flllll...the.......f-f-f-"

"Floor?" I ventured, nearly falling forward as I leaned in to hear the sentence that wasn't coming.

"Entryway," he corrected, and turned around like a snail on roller skates to reach for something on the floor behind the counter.

I found myself breathing hard from the effort of willing the words to come. Davy slapped me lightly on the back with one meaty hand as he went by laughing. The tap sent me sprawling on the floor. While I lay there, imagining ten weeks of this, Mr. OOMP put a yellow tent sign over my head, apparently not noticing I was there. I didn't have to look; I knew what it would say on the outside: Caution, Floor Slippery When Wet. I thought I was gonna cry.

Back on my feet, I joined Davy and Jimmy by the utility closet. They were cracking jokes about the old couple that now held the power to send us to juvenile hall. Seeing that they had no intention of picking up the mop and bucket, I squeezed past and got them myself. When I tried to squeeze back through, the bucket wouldn't fit between them. They didn't move.

"Come on guys, we got to get to work."

"What for?" Davy looked seriously bewildered.

"You heard Mr. Patchani. If we don't do the work, he turns us over to the cops."

"Oh, right. He's gonna call the cops on a

bunch of fifth-graders. Lighten up."

And suddenly it all made sense again, like when he described a homework strike, or when it was just the three of us guys spraying a couple of giggling girls with sprinklers. Yeah, everything was going to be fine.

"Let's terrorize a couple of old farts," said Jimmy, casually as could be.

Suddenly, everything wasn't going to be fine at all. Jimmy and Davy were going to do something stupid, probably beyond stupid, and we were going to be breaking rocks on a prison work gang for the next twenty years.

And oh, they tried to make those old people suffer, but something strange was in the air. Somehow, the old couple seemed oblivious to everything Davy and Jimmy were doing to them. Jimmy gave the mop bucket a swift kick and sloshed water all over the floor right where Old Old Man Peterson was about to walk. The water dried before he could make the three steps necessary to reach it. Lady Undead Mrs. Peterson sent Davy to the storeroom to get coffee cups, and he caught a cockroach, slipped it into a Styrofoam cup, slapped a lid on it, and put it on top of the stack of cups in front of MRS. LUMP. By the time she reached for the cup, the roach had figured out how to lift the cover and had crawled away. Heck, for all I know that roach had evolved into a small mammal before any coffee went into that cup.

Every time the two delinquents tried something, I held my breath. We might not go to jail for breaking a window or a sign, but killing an old person would do the trick. I was standing alone, trying to stop my hands from shaking after another near miss when Mr. Patchani walked up behind me without me noticing.

"Mr. Johnson!" I nearly hit my head on the ceiling when I jumped. "Your special working papers. I didn't collect them earlier."

I dug the paperwork out of my pocket and handed them over. He read the document up and down, then down and up, then he turned it over and held it up to the light. I swear he was reading it again through the paper. Finally, he gave me a look that said, "I know this is a forgery, but I'll hand you over to the authorities later," and walked away.

Mr. Patchani stalked back into his office with nothing more than a grunt. The door closed just before Jimmy switched a salt pourer in for a sugar pourer right by Mrs. LUMP's hand. The customer at the counter asked for sugar in her coffee, and Mrs. LUMP reached for the container. Two minutes later, she had lifted the pourer halfway to the cup of coffee.

"Nevermind," huffed the customer. She grabbed the coffee cup out of Mrs. LUMP's hand, turned on her spiky heals, and stormed out of the shop. Mrs. LUMP was so startled she dropped the pourer which then smashed on the floor.

"B-b-b-boy!" called Mr. OOMP. "Pi-pi-pick ....up.......th-th-that....g-g-g-g-g-gl-gl..."

"Sugar, yeah, I know," I said, and went looking for a broom. I was beginning to wish something bad would happen to get us handed over to the police. My nerves couldn't take much more of this.

Two hours later (it felt like two weeks), the three of us walked out into the fresh air and sunshine. It wasn't enough to pick up my spirits.

"Ten more weeks of that? I don't think I can take it."

Jimmy was eyeing a street sign. Something about how he was looking at that sign made me wonder what he could do to, or with, it that would really cause trouble. I bet he was thinking exactly the same thing. Suddenly he seemed to snap back into the conversation. "What do you mean? That was a blast."

"It was for you. You didn't do any work. All you did was pull stupid pranks. And you!" I turned on Davy. "You must have gone to the bathroom like twelve times. What were you doing in there?"

Davy narrowed his eyes and gave a wicked grin.

"I was taking the seals out of all the pipes. Some of them were a little tricky. I had to work on them for a few minutes at a time so it didn't look suspicious with me being in there for too long."

Davy turned his pocket inside out, showing five rubber rings of different sizes.

"First they'll become leaks, then rivers, then waterfalls!"

Just then, Jimmy noticed a familiar looking piece of paper sticking out of Davy's pocket as well.

"Your working papers! Didn't Mr. Patchani

make you hand them in?"

Davy shook his head. "No, I never got them signed. I just told him I was sixteen and he left me alone."

Twelve years old and he could pass for sixteen. I told myself to remember that next time I needed a "guardian" to get me into a movie.

CHAPTER 7

"Thirty-one, thirty-two, thirty-three…"

Jimmy was looking at his watch, counting the seconds off out loud, tapping his foot, and pumping his hand. I've seen horses that can count with less effort.

"Thirty-four, thirty-five, thirty-six…"

Davy had his mouth wide open, a shiny steel canister pointing down his throat, making a sucking noise that would make a vacuum cleaner proud.

"Thirty-seven, thirty-eight, thirty-nine…"

He was also starting to sway dangerously. When Davy sways, huge shadows block out the sun, weather patterns change, and Volkswagens get out of the way.

"Forty, forty-one…"

Crash! Davy toppled over, bending a wire bagel rack into instant junk.

"A whole can of whipped cream in forty-one seconds; a new world record!" cried Jimmy, arms raised in triumph.

Davy was flat on his back, arms and legs

flopping helplessly, gasping for breath through thick gobs of whipped cream.

I knelt down beside the squirming, beached whale on the floor of the coffee shop. His eyeballs had rolled up into his head.

"What's wrong with him?" Jimmy asked now that he had finished his touchdown dance.

"I think he breathed some whipped cream into his lungs."

"Can he do that?" asked Jimmy, looking more interested than concerned. "I mean, can he do that and live?"

"Not for long. Help me get him up."

Just then, Mr. OOMP stepped out of the men's room. In two steps he would be around the frappe machine and would have a clear view of Davy, sprawled out on the floor. Fortunately, we were able to get Davy to his feet, wipe the whipped cream off his shirt, splash water in his face, dry him off, and comb his hair before the old man made it around the corner. Ten minutes later, Mr. OOMP had managed to walk the twelve feet to the drive through window while we stood trying to look as innocent as we could.

Davy lunged for another can of whipped cream but missed the refrigerator by three feet and ended up on the floor facedown. He was still a little woozy from lack of oxygen. I swear; he almost missed the floor.

Suddenly, Mr. Patchani yelled, "Johnson, get a mop! Every pipe in the men's room has sprung a leak!"

Davy laughed as he sat up, twirling a rubber seal around his middle finger.

"Better hurry up and get that mop, Escapade," Davy called. Sometimes, life just isn't fair.

Welcome to day five. One week down in our sentence, nine more to go. It was Halloween, and not only did we have to work all afternoon, but we had to do it with a couple of zombies. At least if they tried to eat our brains we would be able to run away from them pretty easily.

There really wasn't all that much work to do, and once we learned the routine and didn't have to sit through twenty minutes of instruction for each chore, we had most of the afternoons to ourselves. At least Jimmy and Davy didn't have much to do; I had to hustle just to keep those two from getting into trouble and getting all three of us sent away to juvenile hall.

"Well, I gotta go," announced Jimmy, tossing

his official Joe's House of Joe ball cap over the arm-like steam valve of the espresso machine. It started to hiss ominously and rattle on its legs as the steam built up, a silver cylinder stamping its feet like a spoiled child. I snatched the cap, burning my fingers for my effort. "I get dinner free for my birthday at Steak Through the Heart tonight."

"Ooh, it's 'carve your own cow' night!" Davy's eyes went wide with wonder and delight at the thought of what was advertised as the best restaurant to get a heart attack in all of Belknap County. Then he scrunched his face up in a mockery of concentration.

"Hey, wait a minute. Your birthday is in March." Apparently he got invited to the party last year.

"Not at Steak Through the Heart. My birthday is in October there. It's in August at Taiwan On, June at Pasta Paradise, April at Hog Heaven, December at The Road Kill Road House, February at —"

"Don't they ask for proof?" I asked.

"What proof? It's not like they can check my driver's license; I'm eleven." And with that brilliant display of logic, he grabbed his coat off the rack and headed out the door.

"I'm out of here, too," announced Davy. "It's Halloween, man, places to go, kids to scare, cars to flip. What are you doing tonight?"

"I'm meeting up with Benny. He says he's gonna teach me how they do Halloween in Manhattan, whatever that means." This was my month to make new friends, each of whom was sure to get me in more trouble than the last one.

Davy started to answer, then just smiled, shook his head, and started for the door. "See you in jail," he called over his shoulder.

CHAPTER 8

Benny admitted that his parents never let him go outside at night when they lived in New York, let alone on Halloween. Still, he said, he had heard all the great stories of the tough New York kids. He made this admission as he was packing into his duffle bag dozens of eggs that he had hidden under an old crate behind his house.

"You got to let them ripen at least six or eight weeks," he explained. He had a point. The eggs smelled pretty bad.

"They'll stink to high heavens once they are splattered all over someone's house," I noted admiringly.

"House?" he asked, and broke into an evil grin. Looking back, I should have known where he was headed that night, but right then I was trying to think of anything but Joe's House of Joe.

An hour later the sun had gone down and we had gone up to a wooded hill that overlooked the corner of Main and School Streets.

"It's one point for a wall, five points for a

door, ten points for a window, twenty for the new one."

I looked down. A security light glimmered in the newly replaced picture window on the front of Joe's House of Joe, the same one Jimmy had broken a week ago.

"Oh man, I don't know. I'm in enough trouble with them."

"That's the point! You're slaving away there, and did you do anything wrong? I mean really that bad?"

"Really, it was Jimmy, yeah, but still —"

"Don't they deserve a little payback?"

"I'd feel guilty just looking at the mess tomorrow."

"If it makes you feel better, they'll probably make you clean it up." And with that, he reared back and sent the first egg flying through the air.

Time slowed to a crawl right then. While that egg was in the air, I had a chance to think about a lot of things, about responsibility and character, about actions and consequences, about looking at yourself in the mirror every morning. All those thoughts vanished, of course, when Benny's egg crashed harmlessly in the parking lot, twenty feet from the building itself.

"Rubber arm," I spat and let fly.

Success does tend to wipe out other considerations; that's why people cheat. When my first toss landed dead center, obliterating the picture of the steaming coffee cup on Mr. Patchani's window with a ringing splat, I no longer was aware that there was a tomorrow to face. I was the starting center fielder for the Boston Red Sox and I had just thrown out a runner at home plate.

Benny was jumping up and down with glee. He was so excited, his next throw went wide of the dumpsters.

Mine caught wall. His hit the sidewalk. Window, parking lot, sign, woods, dumpster, parking lot, door, and parking lot again. Benny was missing pathetically, but I was in the zone. I was mesmerized by my own power. Flashing blue lights broke the spell. A police cruiser spun into the parking lot. Motion sensors, I thought, the new security system. I had seen the flashing light panel on the wall behind the counter. It must have called the cops automatically.

"Come on!" I hissed at Benny. But he still had an egg in each hand.

"No," I said, trying to sound authoritative. He smiled. I didn't like that smile, it was too peaceful. Someone who was about to get in that much trouble had no right to smile like that.

"No," I repeated, starting to sound hysterical. What would the cop do? Even if Benny had no chance at all of hitting that cruiser, just throwing an egg near one had to be a federal offense, right?

"NO!" I cried as he let both eggs go in rapid succession. Benny, overweight and as un-athletic as any fifth-grader at Sanbornton Elementary School, with all the time in the world to line up his shots, had missed hitting anything smaller than pavement. Now, under pressure and already moving away from his target, suddenly he was Ken Griffey Junior. The first egg landed in the center of the cruiser's windshield. The stunned cop jumped out of his door and turned in amazement to see the splatter pattern. The second egg caught him square on the back of the head.

Benny was gone while I stood, fear and amazement rooting me to the ground. I didn't do things like this. I wasn't involved in things like this. This was going on my permanent record somehow, I just knew it. All right, I wasn't thinking clearly, but this was all new territory for me. Benny might be used to this kind of situation, but… Benny? Where was he?

I could hear his half-laugh, half-wheeze breaths as he crashed through the woods. The cop heard too and he started up the hill. That got me moving. I turned to follow Benny. Branches hit me in the face. Brambles caught at my clothes. A mud puddle sucked in one of my sneakers. I started to go back for it, but no, it was gone, and the cop was closing in. Nobody's ever finding that sneaker again, I thought. So I ran, bleeding and one-shoed, amazed that I was involved in something like this.

The cop reached the top of the hill; he was thirty yards back. He would catch us, I was sure of it. He reached the mud puddle… and stopped. I saw him over my shoulder. He went down on one knee. Was he tired? Hurt? He looked like he was praying. He looked like he was reaching for –

A branch almost took my head off and I decided I had better pay attention to where I was going. It didn't matter why the cop had stopped. I was free.

CHAPTER 9

The next day I hurried Jimmy and Davy to the coffee shop, knowing I would feel better if we were at least on time. I told them what Benny and I had done and begged them to behave for just one day. We stepped through the door just in time to see Mr. Patchani reach into a paper bag and draw out a mud-covered sneaker. I didn't hear the question; I didn't have to. Both Mr. OOMP and Mrs. LUMP nodded slowly.

That's when Mr. Patchani looked up and noticed me standing there. I don't know how to describe the look he gave me. It was like his nose was trying to burrow into his face at the same time that his brain was tunneling out of his forehead. It wasn't pretty. He breathed in and out, in and out. It got louder and louder with each gasp. He was clearly working up to something, and it was about to come out of his mouth.

Just then, there was a hissing noise that rapidly turned into an ear-splitting whistle.

Jimmy had whipped off his ball cap and tossed it like a Frisbee over the release valve on the espresso machine. Steam was escaping all around the cap, but not enough to release the pressure. The machine began dancing on its short legs. It bounced near the edge of the counter. Mr. OOMP was standing just inches away from the machine. Still, he was barely able to bend forward and put his shoulder into the machine before it tipped off the counter.

Suddenly, Mrs. LUMP shuffled across the linoleum, desperately reaching for a stack of hundreds of Styrofoam coffee cups that were tilting over. Davy had given them a swipe just after Jimmy tossed his ball cap. They fell just as she reached them, but she couldn't close her hands around them in time. They tumbled through her grasp, hitting a portable fan that was set up behind the counter.

The sound was both soothing and disturbing. Soft and gentle, but so strange as to suggest something slightly horrible, like a pigeon hitting a jet engine. The result was probably much like that, too. Little bits of foam filled the air like a sudden blizzard. We were fish swimming in a cloud of white.

For a second, eyes were useless. Then some of the debris must have gotten clogged in the smoke detector because the shop was suddenly filled with a piercing noise. Sprinklers went on and the foam fell to the floor with amazing speed. One second we were lost in a cloud, the next we were soaked and knee-deep in white mush.

Nobody moved. Then the espresso machine

finally wiggled off the counter and exploded against the tile floor. Coffee grounds and hot water hit the foamy mess and erupted in steam and ash.

Now everybody moved. Mrs. LUMP headed for the ladies room. Mr. Patchani dove for his office. Mr. OOMP actually reached out for Davy's neck with his wrinkled, shaky hands.

"What are you guys doing?" I screamed.

"It's a distraction, run!"

"Run where? Why? They know who we are."

"Holy crap, you're right!" yelled Jimmy.

Mr. OOMP spun around like a sleepy turtle. "Watch your mouth, sonny. There are ladies present."

"Yeah, and you're one of them," Davy yelled as he bolted for the door.

CHAPTER 10

The experiment in rehabilitative employment
was over, but fortunately Mr. Patchani was so
mad at Jimmy and Davy that he seemed to have
forgotten all about the egg on his windows.

I grabbed my sneaker as soon as I could so it wouldn't remind him. In the end, he only yelled at me for an hour and told my parents to ground me until I qualified for Social Security, whatever that means. I figure I got off lucky.

That's why I was sitting in my room on the last warm afternoon of the fall, doing my homework with Melinda Trackson. I was forbidden to ever so much as grunt in the direction of "those two Neanderthals," as my mom had put it.

"Do you know what bugs me about all this?" I asked suddenly, picking up a conversation that had taken place in fits and starts all afternoon. "It was the old folks. Once everything settled down, they weren't mad. They just seemed so sad."

"They were disappointed, that's all," said Melinda matter-of-factly, not looking up from the family tree she was working on for the next stage of our 'Living History' project.

"How disappointed could they be? They got stuck with three juvenile delinquents, what did they expect?"

"Did you ever stop to think that maybe they didn't get stuck with you? Maybe having you work off your debts instead of handing you over to the police – which, by the way, you deserved – was their idea?"

The thought, of course, had never crossed my mind.

"THEY kept Mr. Patchani from going to the police? But why?"

Melinda thought about that for a couple of seconds. "Maybe they thought they were doing something good, taking you numbskulls under their wings. They probably don't get to do good things very often at their age, especially with kids. I bet that's why they work at the coffee shop in the first place, to be with younger people."

"At their age, that's all that's left. But I guess I thought they were in it for the money."

"Do you know what they earn per hour? Probably minimum wage."

I looked at her blankly.

"Very…little…money," she said, in exactly the same voice my mom used when she talked to Revelation, back when Revelation was about two.

"You really think they just want to be useful?"

Melinda looked up at me with those huge brown eyes of hers just as wide as they could be. I think she's practicing to be on the U.S. Manipulation Team.

I couldn't look her in the eyes. I looked down at my paper instead, my perfect, white, blank, 'Living History' paper. And then I had an idea. It was a dumb idea, and it would set me up for decades of social death, but it had enough insanity in it to give it a shot.

Picking up the phone right then was probably the hardest thing I've ever done in my life.

"Mr. Peterson," I said, my voice shaking almost as much as his for once, "can I come over and talk to you? I want to ask you to do something for me."

An hour later, I was sitting at my kitchen table, explaining what I had done and who I had done it to.

"Wait a minute," said Mom. "Mr. and Mrs. PETERSON? It can't be the same old couple that…." Her voice trailed off, but I suddenly saw where she was going.

"You mean those are the same people who were working there when you were in school? And they were old then? What was that, forty years ago?"

"It was twenty years ago…I mean, that's none of your business!"

Dad, though, was still focused on what was important.

"If they were, what, ninety then, how old would they be…"

The question hung in the air like the stench of a bad fart.

CHAPTER 11

I thought that Mr. and Mrs. Peterson looked

silly in their Joe's House of Joe uniforms, two

people older than time in brown and yellow

polyester plaid, white tennis sneakers, and visors.

But they walked into Sanbornton Elementary School, he in his bright plaid jacket, purple corduroy pants, black loafers and white socks, and she in a pale sun dress and a hat the size of my family's Thanksgiving turkey (and roughly the same shape, now that I think of it). Standing in a corner of Mrs. Bartgauer's classroom, they looked like aliens on an intergalactic sightseeing tour of Earth. Standing with them, I felt like every pair of fifth-grade eyes was on me. It was not a comfortable way to start the day.

Melinda was there, trying to keep them calm. They had immediately fallen in love with her, of course, when I introduced them to her. I brought Melinda along the afternoon I had asked the couple to come speak to the fifth grade of Sanbornton Elementary School. I wasn't sure then that it was such a great idea, and I was even less sure now, listening to Mr. Peterson trying to speak.

"I-I-I-I-I h-h-h-hope I c-c-ca-ca-can re-re-re-rem-rem…"

"Remember?" Melinda offered.

"…be heard," he continued. "Thi-thi-th-thissss class is s-s-s-s-so l-l-l-l…"

"Energetic?" I offered.

"Exactly!" he said, looking very proud of his communication skills.

Was it too late to take a zero on this project?

Mrs. Bartgauer stood before the class.

Apparently, it was too late.

"Today we have a special treat as part of our Living History project. Escapade has brought us Mr. and Mrs. Peterson, who work at Joe's House of Joe, which we think of as a coffee shop, but it serves many other things. One of which is hot cocoa, and these people are here to tell us some of the folklore of chocolate. You will be expected to be on your best behavior…." She scanned the room, looking at faces that ranged from counterfeit angel to barely restrained demon. When she looked into the eyes of Jimmy Whitehorse she corrected herself. "Better than that, I hope."

At that she turned to the Petersons, a look of desperate apology plastered on her face, then walked to the back of the room and stood directly behind Jimmy's chair. I turned to the two people I was responsible for putting in this position and wondered for a moment who was more likely to kill me when this was over, the Petersons? My classmates? Mrs. Bartgauer? Myself? I shook my head to clear such gloomy thoughts, pulled the corners of my mouth into something that looked like a confident smile, and gave Mr. Peterson a chuck on the shoulder for luck. I then rushed to help Mrs. Peterson pick him up off the floor, brushed him off as best I could, and sat down to wait for my world to end.

Mr. Peterson walked to the center of the floor before the class. On the good side, that took half the period and there was only about 25 minutes of social studies left. On the bad side, it took half the period, and there were only four sets of eyes still looking forward by the time he looked up at the class, mine, Melinda's, and Cherilyn's and Katrina's because they were the ultimate suck-ups and didn't know any other way to act.

But suddenly Mr. Peterson seemed to straighten up. He was taller than I would have guessed. His lips started to move before the sound came out of his mouth, like he was rehearsing the words; no, like he had rehearsed this moment a thousand times.

His eyes glazed. He was no longer there, but was speaking from a place and time far away. The silence changed. It became louder and insistent. Those who had been staring out the window or whispering to their neighbors looked up, and those who had actually been paying attention leaned in, willing the words to come. They jumped back as the sound suddenly broke like water over, no through, a bursting dam.

"The wise men of South America tell us that all men and all animals once came from seeds that the almighty god Sibu kept in large baskets. Sibu guarded the seeds and gave them out sparingly to minor gods to spread upon the earth, where they would grow and live free. Sibu guarded the seeds from the evil gods who wanted to have all living things for themselves. But then one day Sibu desired to travel, to see all the works of his seeds in all the lands. He entrusted his store of seeds to another god, Sura.

"Sura was good and kind but simple and trusting. He planted the seeds and left them unguarded to tend to his maize fields. The evil god Jabaru had been watching and saw his chance. He dug up the seeds and ate them, every one of them. The life-giving seeds made Jabaru feel very powerful, indeed, and he longed to test his great new strength. When poor Sura returned, Jabaru rose up, killed him, and buried him where the seeds had been. Very pleased with himself, Jabaru left the scene and went home to his wives."

"Coooollllll," breathed some of the boys in the class. Mrs. Bartgauer nodded absentmindedly, her face slack, mesmerized by the story. She felt her way blindly to an empty chair in the corner and sat down, chin in her hands, enthralled.

"After a time, Jabaru passed by the place again and saw that two strange trees had sprung up from Sura's grave: a cocoa tree and a calabash. The all powerful god Sibu stood beside the trees. When Sibu saw Jabaru approaching, Sibu asked him to brew a cup of cocoa for him from the tree. Jabaru picked a bean-filled pod and a calabash fruit and took them to his wives, who brewed the cocoa and filled the hollowed out calabash shell with the rich drink. Then Jabaru carried this vessel back to Sibu, holding it out to him.

"'No, you drink first,' all-powerful Sibu insisted politely. Jabaru drank greedily, gulping down the delicious drink as fast as he could. But his delight changed to agony as the cocoa born from Sura's body began to grow inside him. Jabaru's belly began to swell and swell until it burst wide open, spilling out the stolen seeds all over the ground."

"Sibu then placed one of the seeds in Sura's mouth, restoring his friend to life again, and returned the seeds to him so that all humans and animals might one day grow from those precious seeds and enjoy all the gifts that the Earth brings forth."

The class was silent, the first time that had

happened all year in the fifth grade of Sanbornton Elementary School. The old man continued. "As you can tell, cocoa was important to the early South Americans."

"How can you tell that?" asked Benny.

"That is one people's creation story," came a little, clear voice, like a bell tinkling. It was Mrs. Peterson, apparently caught in the same spell as her husband. "They believe cocoa was put there, in the very beginning. It was created before people."

"But why?" asked Cherilyn. "How come a drink was so important?"

"It wasn't just a drink to the early South Americans," replied Mr. Peterson. "And it wasn't the drink we know today. Cocoa back then was brewed with hot peppers. It started fires in men's bellies, like it did to Jabaru in the story. Cocoa was thought to give a man power, confidence, virility!"

Marjorie's hand was up in a second. "What does that mean, virility?"

The old lady smiled a faraway smile and answered. "It means we were drinking hot cocoa the night he first kissed me."

There was a soft "aahhh" from all the girls in the class.

There were various gagging noises from most of the boys.

"We were also drinking cocoa the first time we held hands, and the first time we sat in the balcony of the picture show and –"

She trailed off with a dreamy look in her eyes, and the room sunk into silence. The silence lasted for half a minute before it was broken, predictably, by Jimmy.

"I am never drinking cocoa again," he called out from the back of the room.

"You would if Katrina made it," Benny mumbled just loud enough to be heard by everybody in the class.

Jimmy leapt out of his chair, a heavy math book cocked, aimed at Benny's head, and ready to throw. But Mrs. Bartgauer was on her feet and standing between Jimmy and Benny before Jimmy could let fly. Two months with this class and she was already quicker than she was in September. Jimmy was dragged out into the hallway, protesting loudly that Benny had started it, and the rest of us crowded around Mr. and Mrs. Peterson, peppering them with questions.

"Did people really believe in magic seeds?"

"What exactly is a calabash?"

"Who cleaned up the mess when Jabaru blew up?"

"Do you put pepper in your cocoa at the coffee shop?"

"Would you put it in my mom's cocoa and not tell her?"

Mr. and Mrs. Peterson looked happier than a pig in mud. They tried to answer all the questions that were thrown at them, though at the rate that they were doing it, we would have all been their age before they were done.

CHAPTER 12

When the period was over, and the rest of the class had gone off to music, Mrs. Bartgauer asked me to walk Mr. and Mrs. Peterson out.

"Thank you," I said, still amazed at what had happened. "You were really great."

"D-d-d-d-on't mmmmmmmm-en-men-…"

"Mention it?" I asked, and realized my mistake at once.

"…sound so surprised," he finished.

"Tell FLAB and DOLT we forgive them," added Mrs. Peterson.

"Who and who?" I asked.

"FLAB: Fat Little Annoying Boy, and DOLT: Dirty-mouthed, Obnoxious Little Troublemaker."

It didn't take me long to figure out who they were talking about.

"You gave them nicknames from day one, didn't you?"

"Seems only f-f-f-f-fair," Mr. Peterson stated simply. "You folks like n-n-na-na-nicknames so much, we thought you should have some for yourselves." Then he took his wife's arm and turned towards the door.

Suddenly, it hit me.

"What do you call me?" I asked.

Mrs. Peterson turned to Mr. Peterson and giggled. She giggled. She actually GIGGLED!

"NOBBY."

I thought about not asking, but it would have bugged me for the rest of my unhappy life.

"All right, what's it stand for?"

"The No Backbone Boy of the Year. You shouldn't let other people lead you into trouble."

And with that, Mrs. Peterson swung her Thanksgiving turkey-shaped hat onto her head, giggled again, and spent the next thirty minutes walking out the door.

EPILOGUE

It was the best living history project ever, in the history of the world, and Mrs. Bartgauer gave me a B+. Go figure.

Once the coffee shop got cleaned up again, the "volunteer" jobs there became the most popular after school activity in Sanbornton, New Hampshire. Well, after all, Sanbornton is not the most exciting town on the face of the earth. I would have been happy to continuing working there. As it turns out, Mr. Peterson used to be a professor of folklore and a professional storyteller, and, if you actually bothered to listen to him, he told stories all day long behind the counter. But Mr. Patchani chose Cherilyn and Katrina to fill two of the spots, and the Petersons begged him to give Melinda the other one. That's gratitude for you.

So here it is, a Thursday afternoon in early December, and I am writing stories in my room instead of listening to them at Joe's House of Joe. I heard writers had to suffer for their art, so I guess I should have expected this. And now that this story is done, what do I write next? I still have to write about the moose that ate all the ballots at the last election, but if my mom ever found out where the honey came from, she'd kill me. I guess I'll just have to wait for something interesting to happen to me, Escapade Johnson, the most boring boy in the most boring town in the most boring state in the country, and what chance is there of that?

ABOUT THE AUTHOR

Michael Sullivan is a storyteller, juggler, chess instructor, librarian, and former school teacher who grew up in small town New Hampshire, and now lives in Portsmouth, NH. He has worked with kids in many settings, from summer camps to the Boston Museum of Science, and is rumored to have once been a kid himself. He is the author of the book *Connecting Boys With Books*, and speaks across the country on the topic of boys and reading. In 1998, he was chosen New Hampshire Librarian of the Year.

Visit Michael's website at:
http://www.talestoldtall.com/BoyMeetsBook.html